S0-BPX-998

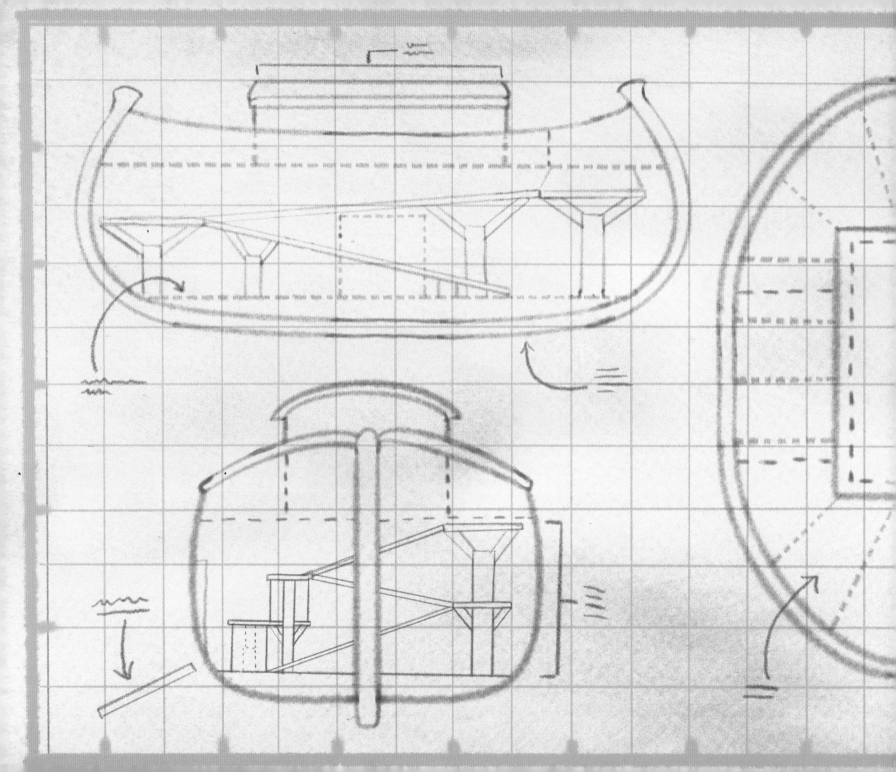

COUNTING ON NAAMAH

A MATHEMATICAL TALE
ON NOAH'S ARK

Written by
Erica Lyons

Illustrated by
Mary Reaves Uhles

INTERGALACTIC Afikoman

SEATTLE

Long before there was an ark or a flood,
there lived a little girl named Naamah.

Though her name meant pleasant (and she was very nice),
Naamah was known best for being clever.

Especially when it came to **MATH**:

When it came to helping her brothers, Naamah's skills were tested times three.

When brother #1 sold his musical instruments, Naamah knew exactly how much to charge. She always subtracted correctly and gave the right amount of change.

She helped brother #2 take care of his flock, figuring out precisely how long it would take to move his herd along, dividing the distance by their speed.

And at archery practice, she could easily show brother #3 how to win.

"Aim a bit to the right and slightly higher," she told him.

It was all about getting the right angle.

Whenever Naamah had a minute to herself, she was busy with projects of her own.

She dreamed up sketches for a desert sand scooter.

She drafted plans for the first automatic camel feeder.

She even came up with a prototype for the world's first life preserver.

But who needed a life preserver in the middle of the desert?

Years later, when Naamah was a young woman, something happened that she hadn't counted on.

Naamah met Noah, who loved numbers also, especially in multiples of two.

Once Noah and Naamah were together, they were impossible to divide, so soon they married. Things were adding up just right.

But then one day, God told Noah and Naamah that there would be a great flood.

To prepare, God told Noah to build an ark.

God told Noah precisely how tall, how wide, and how long it should be.

God told Noah how many floors and what type of wood to use, laying out the entire order of operations.

To Naamah, God simply said,
"I know I can count on you."

So Naamah got right to problem solving.

Naamah counted the number of animals to be housed on each floor.

She factored in their height, their weight, and their temperament too.

She carefully calculated the exact area each animal would need.

The hippos and the elephants needed to be balanced on opposite sides of the boat.

The giraffes needed extra cubits for their necks.

The lions looked hungry, so Naamah knew she couldn't put them near the gazelles.

She arranged and rearranged until all the animals were in the best possible order.

Speaking of hungry animals, there was food to work out.

Naamah knew she needed to multiply the amount of grain and water each animal needed by however long their journey might be.

Would forty days and forty nights be enough?
She planned for extra, just in case...

All the while, Noah worked to build the ark, blueprints spread out.

Looking over his shoulder and then at the pile of gopher wood,
Naamah quickly calculated.

"You didn't buy enough. Looks like we will be 18 planks short."

Back to the store Noah went.

When it came to math, Naamah was always NUMBER ONE.

Soon the rain began to fall.

So Noah, as instructed, rounded up the animals.

Naamah welcomed them all aboard and told them exactly where to go.

Each set of animals moved into a pen that Naamah had measured just right.

Even with all Naamah's precise planning, seven days in, Noah's jokes got old and the animals got restless.

But Naamah had problem solving skills and a higher power on her side. It was simply a matter of regrouping.

The next day, Naamah asked everyone to come up top. It was time for the world's first **DECK-athlon** to begin!

First came the 32-cubit ramp race.

The slope required great speed. The cheetah won, as predicted.

The tortoise's speed was the outlier on the chart.

In the weeks that followed, Naamah hosted many contests of biblical proportions, including…

THE SLINGSHOT.

The final result would be an average of three tries. The giraffe was tall and the elephant was mighty, but the tiny dove swooped in for the win.

"That dove is one to watch," thought Naamah.

WRESTLING.

Sure, the gorilla had strength, but the boa constrictor proved her skill was greater than her size.

And **ARCHERY**, an old favorite of Naamah's. The chimpanzee's opposable digits were a help, but still old eagle's eyes earned her a prime score.

Against all odds, the volume of the seas finally was less than it was the day before.

Even though the rain stopped, it still wasn't time to go. So Naamah announced the next event...

SWIMMING.

The tiger had speed, but he stopped to rest.

So, surprisingly, it was the sloth who proved that she could go the distance.

Naamah quickly tallied the final scores.

It was then that Noah spotted the dove overhead with an olive branch in her mouth.

Land! thought Naamah.

Soon it would come time to rebuild their home, and Noah knew that Naamah would round everyone up and divide all the work.

But first Noah did a quick calculation of his own.
Who had done the most to keep them all afloat?
Noah graphed all the data on a pie chart,
and renamed the ark…

WHAT IS MIDRASH?

A midrash is a tale that begins with a story from the Torah. Then it fills in the missing pieces to imagine the rest. The story of Noah leaves A LOT to the imagination. What was it actually like to live on that ark? How did they take care of all those animals? And who was the generally unnamed "Mrs. Noah"? *Counting on Naamah* tries to answer these questions.

WHO WAS NAAMAH?

According to Jewish tradition, Naamah was the name of Noah's wife. The Hebrew name Naamah literally means pleasant. And yet, isn't that often all that is expected of girls? To be pleasant. But *Counting on Naamah* imagines something much more exciting for Naamah. What if Naamah was truly super-talented at math and inventing? What if much of the success of Noah and the ark was actually due to her?

With five children and two cats, **ERICA LYONS** sometimes feels like she's living on the ark. On land, she's the chair of the Hong Kong Jewish Historical Society and is the Hong Kong Delegate to World Jewish Congress. She's also the founder/director of PJ Library Hong Kong and the author of several books for children. Find her at www.erica-lyons.com.

MARY REAVES UHLES has illustrated *Let's Pop, Pop, Popcorn!*; *A Tuba Christmas*; *The Twelve Days of Christmas in Tennessee*; *The Little Kids' Table*; the *Choose Your Own Adventure Series*, *Beyond the Grave*; and the poetry collection *Kooky Crumbs* by Poet Laureate J. Patrick Lewis. Twice awarded the Grand Prize for Illustration from the SCBWI Midsouth Conference and a finalist in the 2014 Bologna Book Fair Gallery in Bologna, Italy, Mary serves as Illustrator Coordinator for the Society of Children's Book Writers and Illustrators. She lives with her family in Nashville, Tennessee. Find her at www.maryuhles.com.

To Steve, for helping me keep it all afloat.
-E.L.

For the world's creative problem solvers, especially Jess, Susan, Meridth, and Amanda
-M.U.

Text copyright © 2023 by Erica Lyons
Jacket art and interior illustrations © 2023 Mary Reaves Uhles
Designed by Andrew Watson

All rights reserved. No part of this publication may be reproduced, distributed, or transmitted in any form or by any means, including photocopying, recording, or other electronic or mechanical methods, without the prior written permission of the publisher, except in the case of brief quotations embodied in critical reviews and certain other noncommercial uses permitted by copyright law. For permission requests, write to the publisher at the address below.

Intergalactic Afikoman
1037 NE 65th Street, #164
Seattle, WA 98115
www.IntergalacticAfikoman.com

Names: Lyons, Erica, author. | Uhles, Mary, 1972- illustrator.
Title: Counting on Naamah : a mathematical midrash on Noah's ark / written by Erica Lyons ; illustrated by Mary Reaves Uhles.
Description: First edition. | Seattle : Intergalactic Afikoman, [2023] | Interest age level: 004-010. | Summary: Rosie Revere Engineer meets Noah's ark! What if Naamah, Noah's wife, was actually a math and engineering whiz? Enjoy this fun, zany, and girl-powered take on the traditional Noah's ark story.--Publisher.
Identifiers: ISBN: 978-1-951365-18-9 | LCCN: 2022951692
Subjects: LCSH: Women mathematicians--Juvenile fiction. | Women engineers--Juvenile fiction. | Noah's ark--Juvenile fiction. | Noah (Biblical figure)--Family--Juvenile fiction. | Jewish women--Juvenile fiction. | CYAC: Women mathematicians--Fiction. | Women engineers-- Fiction. | Noah's ark--Fiction. | Noah (Biblical figure)--Family--Fiction. | Jewish women-- Fiction. | BISAC: JUVENILE FICTION / Religious / Jewish. | JUVENILE FICTION / Girls & Women. | JUVENILE FICTION / Mathematics.
Classification: LCC: PZ7.1.L965 Co 2023 | DDC: [E]--dc23

Library of Congress Control Number: 2022951692
First Edition
2 4 6 8 10 9 7 5 3 1

Manufactured in China
1-1010531-53574-1/10/2024

1024/B2708/A6

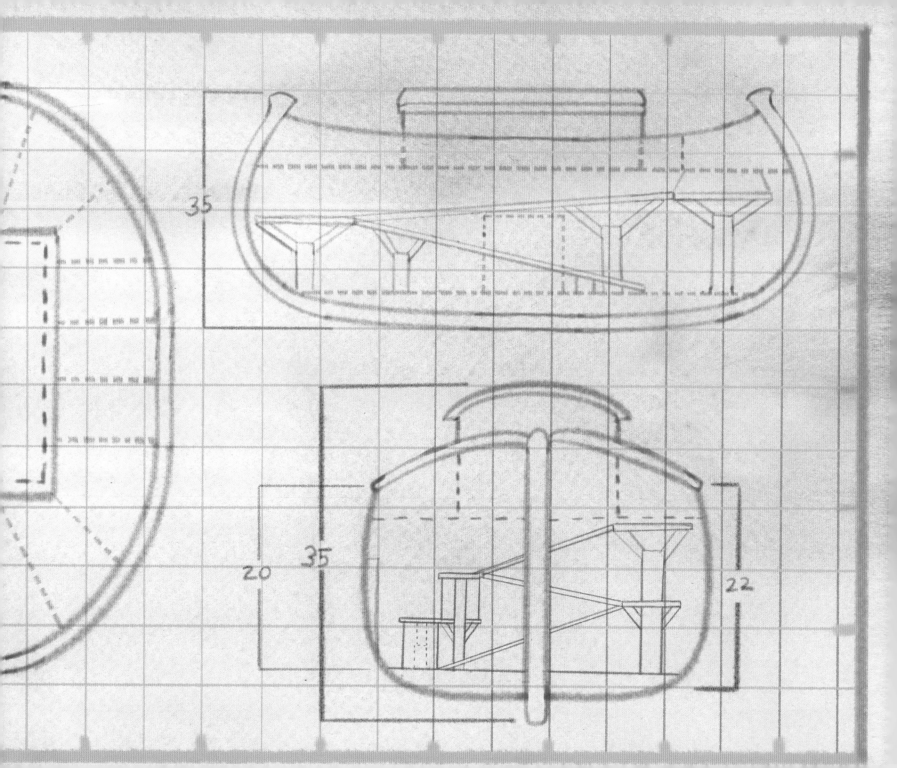